The
Matzah Ball
Fairy

The Matzah Ball Fairy

CARLA HEYMSFELD

illustrated by VLAD GUZNER

UAHC PRESS ❖ NEW YORK

For my mother, Jane Raskin,
and my Aunt Sadie, who both made
perfect matzah balls every time
Carla Heymsfeld

For my children, Mitya and Masha
Vlad Guzner

One by one, Frieda Pinsky dropped her matzah balls into the big pot of chicken soup. It was the first night of Passover and the whole Pinsky family was coming to Frieda's house for the seder.

"Please be light and fluffy," she pleaded as she stirred the matzah balls around the soup. "Please puff up and float." But the matzah balls just sat on the bottom of the pot like dozens of little stones.

Suddenly a soup bubble popped and splashed, and a tiny, plump woman appeared next to Frieda's stove. Startled, Frieda jumped. Her soup ladle flew from her hand, pitching a matzah ball onto the counter with a wet thud.

The tiny woman pointed a dimpled finger at the round lump.

"You call that a matzah ball?" she gurgled.

"Who are you?" Frieda asked, now more amazed than frightened.

"I'm the Matzah Ball Fairy." The woman sounded as if she were speaking through water. "I came in through the soup."

As Frieda stared openmouthed, first at her soup pot and then at the fairy, the little woman poked the matzah ball with her foot and said, "Like lead, isn't it?"

Frieda frowned. "A real fairy would help, not make fun."

"But, of course, I'll help. That's why I'm here." The woman pulled a small envelope from her pocket. "Here." She pushed it into Frieda's hand. "A pinch of this and the matzah balls at your seder will be the lightest, fluffiest matzah balls anywhere."

Real magic. Frieda couldn't wait. Holding the precious envelope in one hand, with the other she grabbed matzah meal, eggs, and oil and measured them into a bowl.

The fairy watched as Frieda began to add the powdery grains of magic. "Be careful," she warned. "Use only one pinch."

Frieda nodded, but she wasn't really listening. She didn't even hear the Matzah Ball Fairy splash back into the soup pot.

Frieda blended the magic powder into the batter. It made her spoon cut through the thick mixture as if it were whipped cream. "If one pinch is this good," Frieda said to herself, "imagine how wonderful my matzah balls would be if I used a little more."

And she stirred in
two more pinches
of the magic powder.

That night, all the Pinskys gathered

around Frieda's table for the seder.

When it was time for the soup, Uncle Solly's eyes opened very wide. So did his mouth. He gobbled up four of Frieda's matzah balls and asked for another. "These are the lightest, fluffiest matzah balls I have ever tasted," he said as he patted his stomach.

"Solly's absolutely right," agreed the Pinskys from Vermont, taking second helpings. "They taste lighter than air."

"Indeed," nodded the Pinskys from Florida as they held out their soup bowls for more.

Even the Philadelphia Pinskys, who usually didn't eat much, asked for seconds.

Frieda beamed as she watched her family eat. But then something very odd happened.

Uncle Solly began to rise.

At first it was only an inch or so, but soon he was hovering over the dining room table like a plump helicopter. "Get me down," he shouted.

The Vermont Pinskys grabbed at his legs, but instead of pulling him down, they began to float up, too.

As they circled the chandelier, the Florida Pinskys, squealing loudly, joined them.

"What's going on?" Uncle Daniel asked as he bounced gently along the ceiling.

"It's those matzah balls," Uncle Solly said. "They were too light and fluffy."

"And you ate too many of them," his wife scolded. Having eaten only one, she was floating only a couple of feet off the floor.

The younger Pinskys swooped about trying to catch each other. "This is fun!" they shrieked as they flew down the hall.
"Get down this instant," their parents ordered. But it was hopeless. The whole family was floating around Frieda's house as if they were matzah balls in a pot of chicken soup.

"Just how much powder did you put in the matzah balls?"
a gurgly voice whispered in Frieda's ear.

"Oh, thank heaven you're here!" Frieda cried. "Help us. How can I get everyone back down?"

The fairy chewed her lip as she considered the problem. "They are floating," she explained, "because they ate something lighter than air. To come down, they have to eat something heavy."

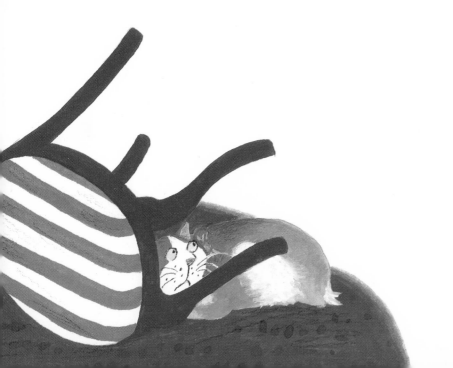

She looked around the kitchen. Her eyes lit up when she saw a pan filled with Frieda's potato kugel.

"There is your answer," she said, pointing to the pan. "Your potato kugel will do it. Give everyone a little of that, and they'll come down."

Frieda cut the kugel into pieces — one for each floating Pinsky in the house. She dragged her kitchen stool into the dining room, stood upon it like a traffic officer, and as her relatives floated past, handed out the kugel.

It worked! One bite of kugel and each flying Pinsky bumped back to the ground.

"This was a most remarkable Passover,"
Uncle Solly said when it was all over.
"Tell me, what did you put in those
matzah balls?"

Everyone listened as Frieda told them about her visit from the Matzah Ball Fairy. When she finished, Frieda looked around at her astonished family and said, "I didn't mean to cause all this trouble. I just wanted to make light, fluffy matzah balls."

"Why didn't you ask me?" Grandmother Pinsky asked from the big armchair. "I taught everyone in this family to make matzah balls, and I would have taught you, too."

"Oh," said Frieda.

"It's not too late. Come see me tomorrow. Together we'll make matzah balls like magic, but without magic."

And they did.

Postscript

Passover is the holiday during which Jewish people celebrate their escape from slavery in Egypt. Because the enslaved Jews left Egypt in a big hurry, they did not have time to let their bread rise.

Today, during Passover, Jewish people eat only unleavened bread — matzah — in memory of the bread their ancestors took with them thousands of years ago.

In many families matzah balls, which are dumplings made with matzah meal, eggs, and fat, are a traditional part of the holiday feast.

About the Author

Carla Heymsfeld, an elementary school reading specialist, has published three books for children and two books for teachers, including the award-winning *Coaching Ms. Parker* (Scarsdale, NY: Bradbury Press, 1992). She resides in Reston, Virginia.

About the Illustrator

Vlad Guzner, a successful illustrator of children's books in his native Russia, has illustrated for the prestigious *New York Times Book Review* among other publications and *A Thousand and One Chickens* for the UAHC Press.